What's happening at the seaside?

Heather Amery
Illustrated by Stephen Cartwright

Consultant: Betty Root

Building a sandcastle

Everyone is doing something to help build the sandcastle.
Who is digging the moat?

Which bucket made the top of the castle?
How many flags are there?

In the sea

How many children are wearing snorkels?
Who is learning to swim?

Who doesn't like being in the water?
How many seagulls are there?

Having a picnic

How many children are eating sandwiches?
Who is wearing sunglasses?

Who is getting cold?
Who is being naughty?

Playing in the rock pool

How many crabs can you see?
Who is about to fall into the water?

How many red buckets are there?
Who is collecting shells?

On the jetty

How many children are fishing?
What has the girl in the striped top caught?

What are the cats waiting for?
Who has lost her hat?

At the ice cream stand

How many birds can you find?
Who has a cold head?

Which children have pink ice creams?
What other kinds can they buy?

Time to go home

Everyone seems to have lost something.
Who is looking for his pipe? Can you see where it is?

Can you help the others find a missing shoe, a paddle, a sandal, a sock and a flipper?

Getting dressed

Who do all these things belong to?

First published in 1984 by Usborne Publishing Ltd., Usborne House, 83-85 Saffron Hill, London EC1N 8RT, England. www.usborne.com
Copyright © 2005, 1992, 1984 Usborne Publishing Ltd. First Published in America 1993. This edition Published in America in 2006.